P9-DTB-269

NO LONGER PROPERTY OF
SEATTLE PUBLIC LIBRARY

For my brother, Geoff, who
throws the best parties
—M.P.

To my parents, for their
love and support
—M.C.

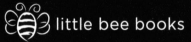 little bee books

An imprint of Bonnier Publishing USA
251 Park Avenue South, New York, NY 10010
Text copyright © 2017 by Miranda Paul
Illustrations copyright © 2017 by Maggie Caton
All rights reserved, including the right of reproduction in whole or in part in
any form. LITTLE BEE BOOKS is a trademark of Bonnier Publishing USA,
and associated colophon is a trademark of Bonnier Publishing USA.
Manufactured in China LEO 1116
First Edition 10 9 8 7 6 5 4 3 2 1
Library of Congress Cataloging-in-Publication Data
Names: Paul, Miranda, author. | Caton, Maggie, illustrator.
Title: Blobfish throws a party / by Miranda Paul; illustrated by Maggie Caton.
Description: New York: Little Bee Books, [2017] | First edition.
Summary: Longing for friends and hungry for delicious treats, a fish who lives
near the bottom of the ocean invites everyone to a party, with unexpected results.
Identifiers: LCCN 2016014969
Subjects: | CYAC: Fishes—Fiction. | Friendship—Fiction. | Parties—Fiction. | Humorous stories.
Classification: LCC PZ7.1.P3852 Bl 2017 | DDC [E]—dc23
LC record available at https://lccn.loc.gov/2016014969

ISBN 978-1-4998-0422-5

littlebeebooks.com
bonnierpublishingusa.com

BLOBFISH THROWS A PARTY

by **Miranda Paul**

illustrated by **Maggie Caton**

little bee books

Blobfish lived at the bottom of the ocean.

The dark, lonely bottom of the ocean.

With no lights.
No friends.
And no delicious treats.

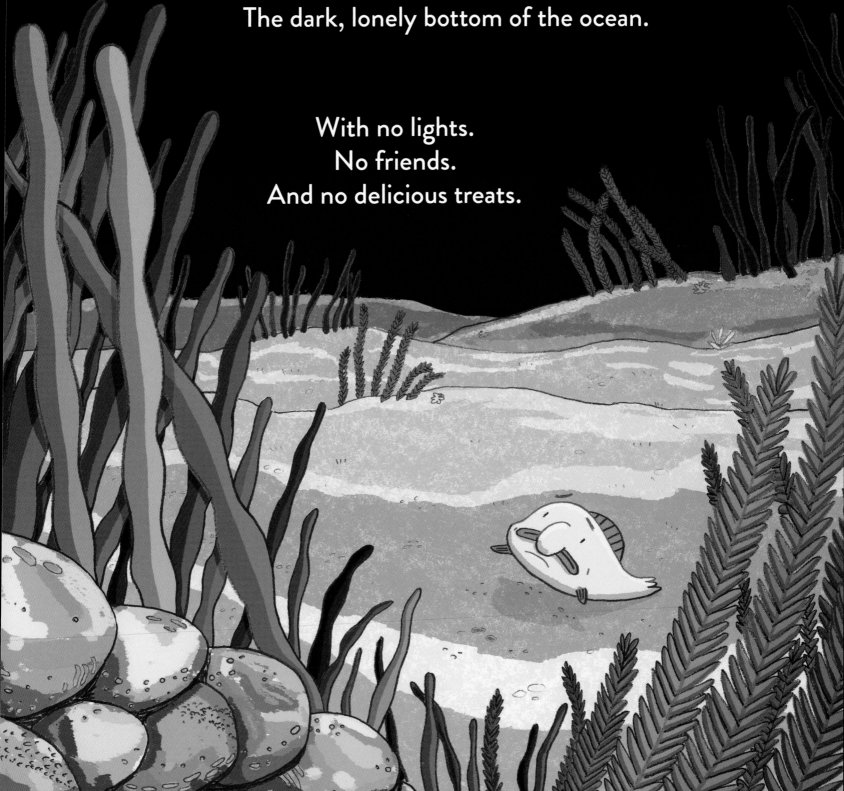

Blobfish wanted lights. And friends. And definitely treats.
He could think of only two ways to get these things:

1. Throw a party.

2. Save the world in true hero style.

(Heroes always got whatever they wanted. Or so he'd heard.)

After thinking it over, he decided on Option #1.
So Blobfish called out:

DEEP-SEA PARTY!

BRING A TREAT TO SHARE!

But the mermaids heard...

"Cheap, free party! Sling on a sheet to wear!"

And the shorebirds heard...

"Cheep-peep party!
Sing and tweet with flair!"

And the monkeys heard...

"Creepy tree party!
Wring and eat your hair!"

And the farm animals heard...
"Sheep tea party!
Spring and meet at the fair!"

And the farmers heard...
"Keep up the party!
Ring a beat to blare!"

And the dancers heard...
"Be really arty! Swing your feet in the air!"

And the kids heard...
"Be a smarty! Fling your **UNDERWEAR!**"

As the message passed on and on, the entire planet grew wacky and wild. Everyone was partying in loud, weird ways.

Except Blobfish.
He was still alone.

With no lights. No friends. No delicious treats.
Blobfish thought it couldn't get worse, but then...

"Eeeew! Earthlings are disgusting! And loud. Their candy isn't worth it.

ABORT THE MISSION!"

CANDY

CANDY

CANDY

"Blobfish?"

"BLOBFISH!"

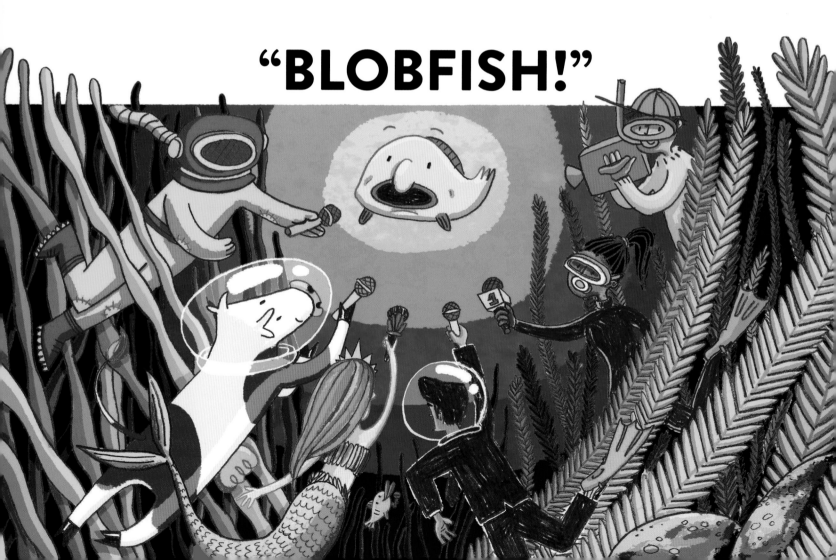

"YOU SAVED THE WORLD IN TRUE HERO STYLE!"

Blobfish was never alone again.

He had plenty of sparkly things to brighten the dark,
and plenty of visitors to keep him company.

And thanks to the grateful candy store owners of planet Earth, Blobfish enjoyed a lifetime supply of delicious treats.

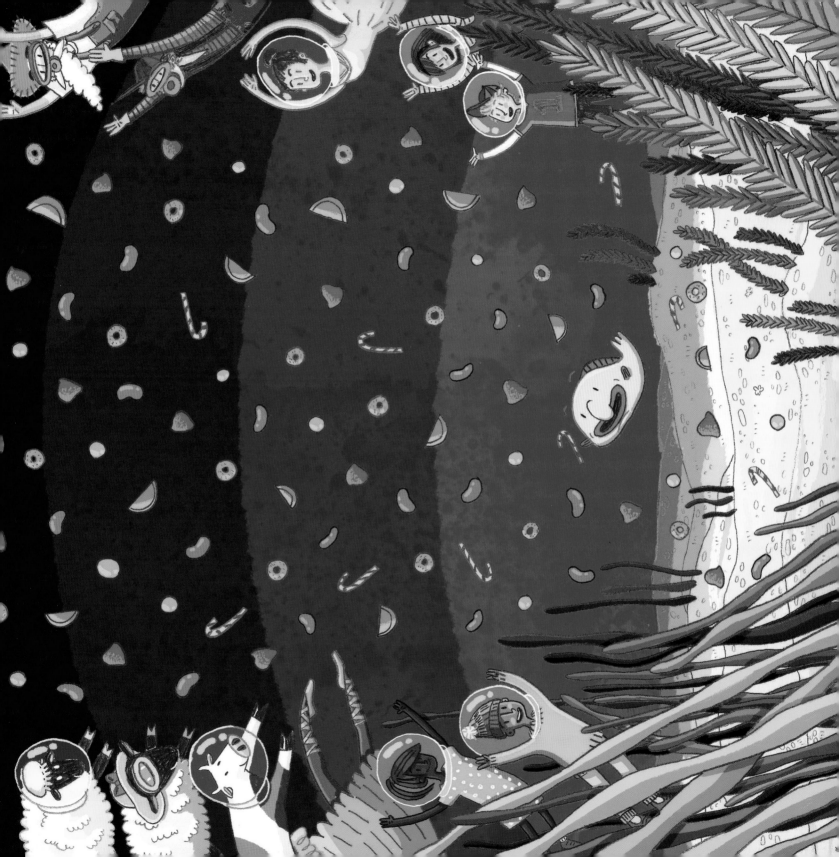

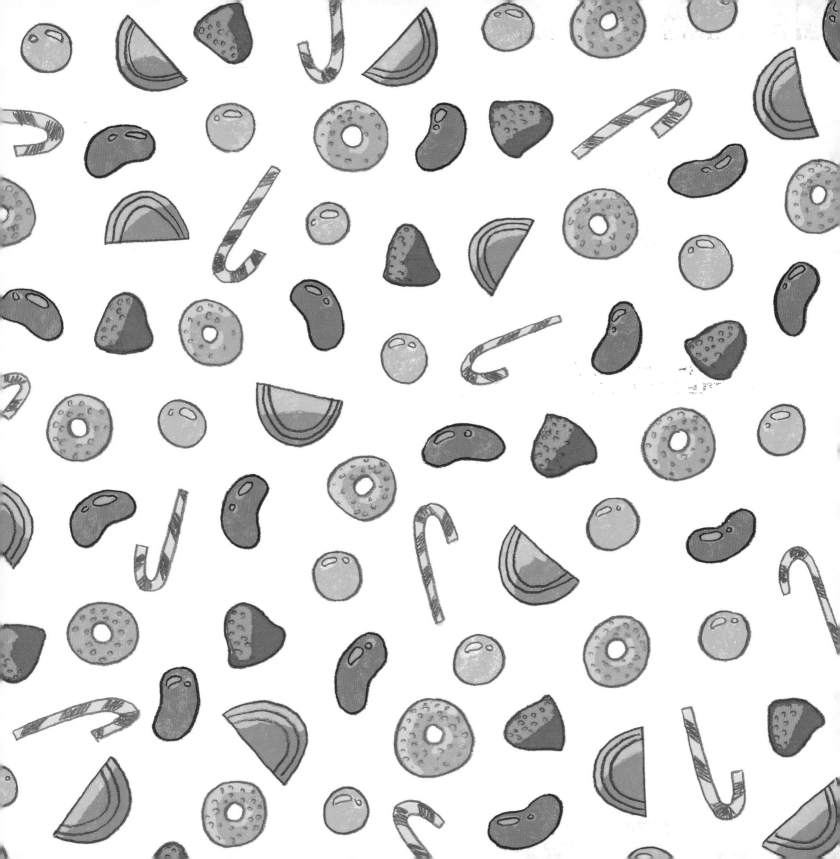